In fond memory of
Harry and Mandy,
Roo, Chiquita and Steve

PUFFIN BOOKS

Published by the Penguin Group: London, New York, Australia, Canada, India, Ireland, New Zealand and South Africa
Penguin Books Ltd, Registered Offices: 80 Strand, London WC2R 0RL, England

puffinbooks.com

First published 2007
1 3 5 7 9 10 8 6 4 2
Text and illustrations copyright © Harry Horse, 2007

Paperback ISBN: 978-0-140-56963-6
Hardback ISBN: 978-0-141-38043-8

Little Rabbit's Christmas

HARRY HORSE

One Christmas Eve, when the snow lay all around,
Little Rabbit saw something that he really liked.
"Look, Papa! A beautiful sledge!"
Papa agreed that it was a lovely sledge.

When they got home, Little Rabbit told his Mama all about the sledge.

"It is red," said Little Rabbit, "and it goes

Whoosh!"

Mama asked Little Rabbit to help his brothers and sisters decorate the Christmas tree. But Little Rabbit did not want to . . .

Instead he watched the snow falling outside the burrow.

"I wish I had a sledge," he sighed.
"Then I could go on the snow."

That night, Mama tucked Little Rabbit up in bed and read him a story.

She told Little Rabbit that if he was good the Christmas Rabbit would leave some lovely presents in the stocking at the end of his bed.

"Will he bring me a sledge?" wondered Little Rabbit.

He did not think that the red sledge could fit in such a little stocking.

"Go to sleep, Little Rabbit," said Mama.

"Who knows what the Christmas Rabbit will bring?"

"Wake up, Little Rabbit, it's Christmas morning!" cried his brothers and sisters. Little Rabbit was very excited.

He looked in his stocking.

He found a bouncy blue ball,
a yo-yo, a pair of mittens . . .

but no sledge.

"Where's my sledge?" said Little Rabbit.

Little Rabbit went to look under the
Christmas tree to see if the sledge was there.
Then he looked up the chimney
to see if it had got stuck.

He even looked under Mama and Papa's bed.

"It's not fair," cried Little Rabbit. "I only wanted a sledge."

"Dry your eyes, Little Rabbit, and look outside," said Papa.

It was the red sledge! Little Rabbit was so happy.

"The Christmas Rabbit has been," he told everyone.

"And he brought me a sledge!"

Papa tied a string on the sledge so that Little Rabbit could pull it across the snow.

"Put your mittens on," said Mama. "It's cold outside."

"Mittens are for babies, Mama," said Little Rabbit. And off he ran, pulling the red sledge behind him.

Everybody loved the red sledge.

"It's mine," said Little Rabbit. "The Christmas Rabbit brought it for me."

Molly Mouse wanted to go on the sledge
but Little Rabbit would not let her.

"You're too small," he said.
"You might fall off and
hurt yourself."

Benjamin and Rachel
wanted to sit on
the sledge.

"You are too big and
you might break it,"
said Little Rabbit.

Little Rabbit did
not want to play
with Benjamin's tool
box, Rachel's painting
set or Molly Mouse's
snowshoes.

"It's not fair," said Little Rabbit.
"Everybody wants to play with my sledge!"

So Little Rabbit took the sledge far away
to where he could play with it alone.

Little Rabbit climbed up a hill.

Whoosh!

Down the hill he flew.

"Look at me!" he cried.
But nobody was looking.

"I'll show them how fast I can go and then they'll see," said Little Rabbit.

So he climbed the biggest hill he could find.

Whoosh! went the red sledge.
Down the hill he flew.
Faster and faster.

"Look out!" cried Little Rabbit. The sledge was going too fast.
He flew through a hedge, over a frozen stream and then . . .

. . . Crash!

Little Rabbit flew off
and landed in the snow.

The red sledge was broken.

Little Rabbit climbed back up the hill, dragging
the broken sledge behind him.

It was such a long way back up to the top. His nose got cold.
His little paws got colder. He wished that he had worn his mittens.

The snow got deeper.
Little Rabbit got stuck in a snowdrift.

"Help!" cried Little Rabbit. "I'm stuck!"

"Don't worry," said Molly Mouse. "I'll help you out with my new snowshoes. Hold on."

And she pulled Little Rabbit out of the snow.

Benjamin and Rachel came along. They looked at the red sledge.

"It's broken," said Little Rabbit. "And it's all my fault."

"I'll mend it with my new tools," said Benjamin.
"I'll paint it with my new paint brushes," said Rachel.
Little Rabbit was so happy.

When the sledge was mended, Little Rabbit's friends helped pull the sledge back up the hill.

When they got to the top they all climbed on to the sledge.

"Hold on!" said Molly Mouse, and off
down the hill they flew.

"Look at us!" cried Little Rabbit. It was the best fun he had ever had.

"Again!" cried Little Rabbit.

They played all day long on the sledge till the sun set over the snowy fields.

Little Rabbit took his friends home for a Christmas party.

Little Rabbit helped Papa light the Christmas candles and they danced round the tree and sang carols.

They played games and ate delicious food.

When Little Rabbit's friends had gone home,
Papa carried him to bed.

"Whoosh . . ." said Little Rabbit sleepily. "Christmas is
good, Papa, but sharing it with friends is even better."